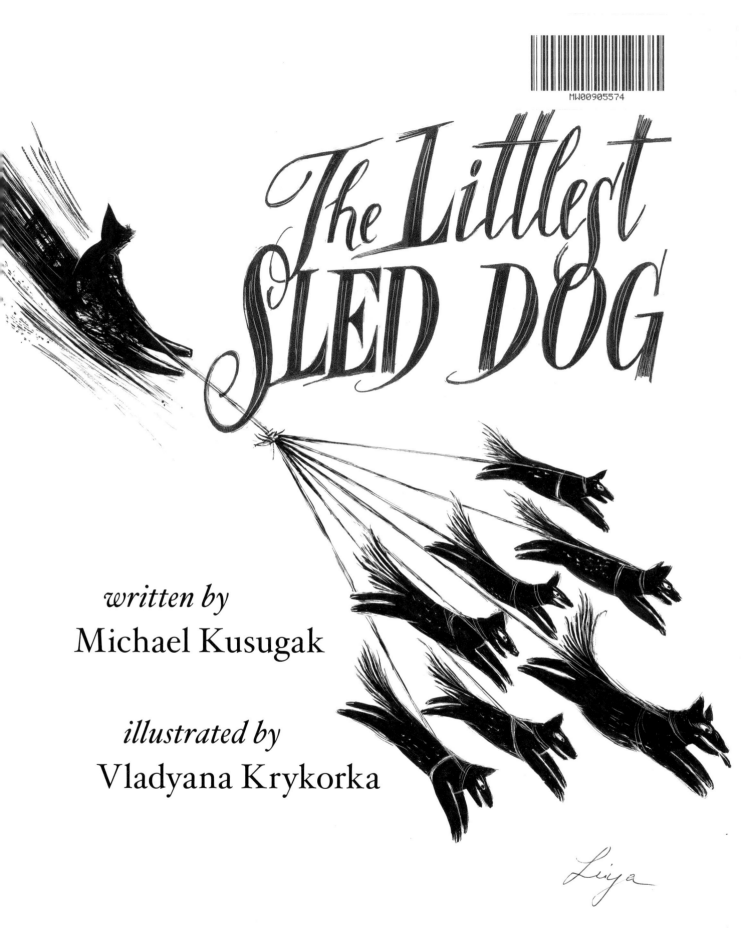

The Littlest SLED DOG

written by
Michael Kusugak

illustrated by
Vladyana Krykorka

ORCA BOOK PUBLISHERS

Library and Archives Canada Cataloguing in Publication

Kusugak, Michael
The littlest sled dog / written by Michael Kusugak ; illustrated by Vladyana Krykorka.

ISBN 978-1-55143-752-1(bound).--ISBN 978-1-55469-174-6 (pbk.)

I. Krykorka, Vladyana II. Title.

PS8571.U83L48 2008   jC813'.54   C2008-902684-5

First published in the United States, 2008
Library of Congress Control Number: 2008927290

Summary: A little dog named Igvillu dreams of being a sled dog in the North.

Orca Book Publishers gratefully acknowledges the support for its publishing programs
provided by the following agencies: the Government of Canada
through the Book Publishing Industry Development Program and the Canada Council
for the Arts, and the Province of British Columbia through the
BC Arts Council and the Book Publishing Tax Credit.

Cover artwork by Vladyana Krykorka
Design by Teresa Bubela

ORCA BOOK PUBLISHERS   ORCA BOOK PUBLISHERS
PO Box 5626, STN. B   PO Box 468
VICTORIA, BC CANADA   CUSTER, WA USA
V8R 6S4   98240-0468

www.orcabook.com
Printed and bound in China

12 11 10 09 • 4 3 2 1

For Dylan Mikilaaq
Sangikti Kusugak,
my grandson. M.

For Petra Mila,
my granddaughter,
with all my love. V.

Igvillu is a Dog.

She was born in Red Deer, Alberta.
When she was a puppy, her mother
told her stories. What do dogs
tell stories about? Other dogs, of
course. Igvillu's mother told her
stories about dogs from all
around the world.

Her mother said, "There are huge dogs called St. Bernards. They live in the mountains. Sometimes it snows. It snows and it snows. The snow piles up until it is so high it cannot pile up any higher. Then it rolls down the mountainsides, burying everything in its way. Sometimes it buries skiers. Then these huge dogs run out on the snow. They sniff and sniff. They find the skiers and dig them up. They are amazing dogs."

Igvillu said to herself, "When I grow up, I am going to be a St. Bernard."

She dreamed about running in the deep, pure-white snows of the Alps and rescuing skiers.

She dreamed of running, running so fast, chasing wolves with sleek Irish wolfhounds. She dreamed of hunting with dingoes in Australia. She dreamed of splashing in clear waters, fetching ducks with golden retrievers.

But most of the time she dreamed about pulling huge heavy sleds with big huskies, way up north. She would be called Fang or something cool like that. She and the other dogs would weave through snowy trees, with someone yelling "Mush, mush!" behind them. That was her favorite dream.

"Time to eat!" the people at Igvillu's kennel yelled.

But Igvillu just lay there, daydreaming, until someone saw her and shouted, "You too!" After a time, they just called her You-too, not Fang.

One day, the owners of her kennel said, "You-too, you are going way up north. You are going to a place called Rankin Inlet, in Nunavut." And that is what she did. She went to live with a storyteller, way up north in northern Canada.

You-too and the storyteller spent their spring
and summer at a cabin, fishing on the shore of
the mighty Hudson Bay. In spring, they fished
through long cracks in the sea ice. The ice was
cold. You-too shivered. Her master picked her
up and carried her in his coat. She was only little.
When the ice went away, her master set nets in
the tidal waters and caught silver, shimmery,
slippery, flippery fish called Arctic char.

It was a wondrous place. There were no
trees. But there were plenty of huge rocks to
run around. There were siksiks to chase, those
ground squirrels that were half her size. You-too
loved it at the cabin. She ran here and there and
everywhere, exploring, all day long.

In the community of Rankin Inlet, she had to walk on a leash. She pulled and pulled. "I am practicing," she said to herself. "I am going to become the mightiest sled dog in the world. I will pull big sleds over deep snow all day long."

They did not call her Fang here either. They called her Igvillu (they pronounced it "ig" as in fig, "vill" as in will and "lou" as in you: Ig vill lou), which in Inuktitut means "you too."

To get out to their cabin, her master drove a four-wheeler, a motorcycle with four balloon tires. Igvillu ran alongside until she got too hot and tired. Then her master picked her up and put her in a special backpack for carrying babies. Igvillu bounced up and down in the backpack. She fell asleep and dreamed she was on a sled bouncing over the snowdrifts out on the sea ice.

One day it began to snow. It snowed and snowed. Igvillu whined. Her master said, "Do you want to go outside?"

Every day she whined to go out to pee and anaq. The snow was cold. When her paws got cold, she lifted them up, one after the other, trying not to keep them on the snow too long. Sometimes she tried to lift all her paws up in the air at the same time, but she only fell over. Her master bought little bootees for her. When she wanted to go out to pee and anaq, she lay down on her back with her paws sticking up, waiting for her master to put her bootees on her paws.

Every night she fell asleep in her little
bed on the floor in the bedroom. Early in the
morning she would jump up on her master's
big bed. She would curl up on the soft down
covers at the foot of the bed and go back to
sleep. Before she knew it, she was dreaming
about being a huge lead dog, leading her charges
across the frozen snows.

One day, when she was out walking with her master, she saw them, real sled dogs. They were huge. They had thick scruffy fur. There were black ones, brown spotted ones and others of many colors. The lead dog was big and gray. Eskimo dogs, they are called. They had harnesses on, and they were pulling a huge sled with two runners.

Their master did not yell "Mush!" He only said, in a low voice, "Auva ih, uai-uai, hut, hut... hut, hut."

Igvillu heard the lead dog call to the other dogs, "Right! Slow, slow...Carefully now. Left, left..."

They were magnificent. Igvillu followed them in her little bootees, pulling her master behind her, running as fast as she could.

The big dogs stopped. Their master took them out of their harnesses and tied them to a long chain along the ground. He opened a big wooden box. The box was full of huge chunks of frozen fish. He picked up handfuls of the fish and threw them at the dogs. "Here you are, Gray," he called. "Here, Crooked-runner; here's yours, Slow-puller; and yours, Off-course..."

They had strange names, these dogs. Not one of them was called Fang.

The big dogs gulped their fish down whole, hardly chewing on them at all. "More! I want more!" they growled. They snarled. They snapped their jaws at each other like alligators. They fought. They stole each other's fish. Igvillu wagged her tail. She pulled her master toward the lead dog, the big gray one.

Gray lunged at Igvillu, stopping only when he reached the end of his line. The big dog bared his fangs and warned, "Growwl! Stay away from my food or I will eat you up, your little bootees and all."

Igvillu jumped back. She pulled her master away from the line of dogs and dragged him as fast as she could, yelping, all the way home. Oh, she was scared! Behind her, she could hear Gray laugh, "Heh, heh, heh..."

That night, after supper, Igvillu climbed
onto the back of the sofa. Her master was
watching a movie on television, her very favorite
movie.

Igvillu looked out the window at the dark,
windy, snowy night. She thought about the big
dogs outside. They did not have bootees on.
They were not in a warm house, curled up on
a sofa. They were out there, curled up in the
cold snow with the wind howling around them.
With that shivery thought in her mind, she
fell asleep.

And in her sleep, she dreamed.

This time she did not dream about sled
dogs. She dreamed about the girl in the movie.
The girl was walking along a yellow brick road.
She was singing so beautifully, a song about
rainbows, and dreams coming true. The girl
had a little dog that looked just like Igvillu.
Igvillu dreamed about the dog and thought,
"I'm not going to be a sled dog after all.
I'm going to be a movie star."

Taimakalauq

AFTERWORD

The Littlest Sled Dog is my ninth book with Michael Kusugak. My life changed in 1987 when I illustrated *A Promise Is a Promise* and first met Michael at the book's launch party. Never having been to the Arctic, I was worried that I had not been able to capture its true majesty. I was overjoyed to learn that Michael was happy with my illustrations. Meeting him was like meeting an old friend.

We have worked closely on all our books together, and I have visited the Arctic six times to do research and to see the great North for myself. Getting to know this part of Canada has truly enriched my life—my affection and admiration for the Inuit, their culture and their land has grown with each book.

Every time Michael visited Toronto, he came to my home. Our family always had a dog, one of three cairn terriers. And since Michael likes dogs, they liked him too. He enjoyed their spunky jolly nature and scruffy look, and his question was always "I wonder how this dog would like it up North." Finally, just a few years ago, he got his answer when Igvillu, a cairn terrier puppy, came to live with him in his home in Rankin Inlet. Igvillu loves her life with her master; she must be the only cairn (a breed native to Scotland) north of sixty!

My third cairn, Myshka, died not long ago, but he lives on in all the books that I have illustrated. I sneaked him into every one of them. He was the best model an artist could wish for—just like Igvillu!

Vladyana Krykorka, 2008
(P.S. "Krykorka" in Inuktitut means "seaweed"!)